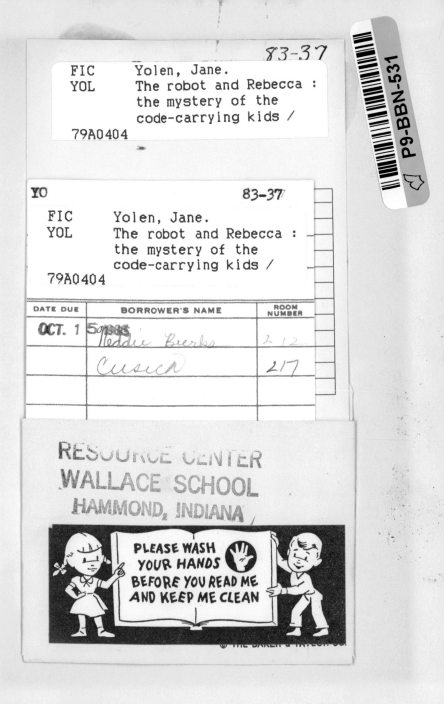

PLEASE WASH
YOUR HANDS
BEFORE YOU READ ME
AND KEEP ME CLEAN

© THE BAKER & TAYLOR CO.

THE ROBOT AND REBECCA

The Mystery of the
Code-Carrying Kids

Jane Yolen

illustrated by Jürg Obrist

Alfred A. Knopf ▪ New York

Other Knopf Capers books
Published by Alfred A. Knopf, Inc.

Man from the Sky by Avi
Rosie's Double Dare by Robie H. Harris
Running Out of Time by Elizabeth Levy
The Case of the Weird Street Firebug by Carol Russell Law
The Mystery on Bleeker Street by William H. Hooks

The text of *The Robot and Rebecca* was originally published
by the Random House Student Book Club.

2 4 6 8 9 10 7 5 3 1

Library of Congress Cataloging in Publication Data

Yolen, Jane H   The robot and Rebecca.
The Mystery of the Code-Carrying Kids (Capers)
Summary: Rebecca uses the robot she receives for her ninth
birthday to solve a mystery in Bosyork, biggest metroplex of
the East Coast of America in 2121. [1. Mystery and detective
stories. 2. Robots—Fiction. 3. Science fiction] I. Title.
II. Series. PZ7.Y78Ro   1980   [Fic]   79-27391
ISBN 0–394–84488–2   ISBN 0–394–94488–7 lib. bdg.

This book is for
SUE ALEXANDER
who sure could use
at least one robot to help

Contents

THE ROBOT AND REBECCA

▄▌▌ ▄▌▌ ▄▌▌ ▄▌▌

The Mystery of the
Code-Carrying Kids

1

The Birthday Present

On July 1, 2121, Rebecca Jasons was nine years old.

The apartment-city loudspeakers sang happy birthday to her.

Happy birthday from your city,
May your day be full of glitter.
Just be sure your door is bolted,
Curb your dog, pick up your litter.

Rebecca made a face at the loudspeaker over her bed. She didn't even have a dog. It just went to prove that the city didn't know everything. The speakers sang that song to everyone who had a birthday on July 1—boys and girls, men and women, and any aliens who lived in Bosyork. That was the biggest metroplex on the East Coast of America.

But Rebecca smiled anyway. She sat up and counted the presents at the foot of her bed. There were three big boxes. She hoped that in one of them was the present she *really* wanted.

The first present she opened was from her mother. It was a solar-powered cycle.

"Bother," said Rebecca. Her mother was a machine nut. Their apartment was already full of motorized things. A solar cycle was not what Rebecca wanted. There was very little direct sun in the city. And, besides, Rebecca preferred walking.

The second present she opened was from her father. It was a doll that burped, said

"Excuse me," had nightmares, and cried itself to sleep.

"Double bother," said Rebecca. Her father had this *thing* about dolls. He gave them to everybody. Well, Rebecca had a thing about dolls, too. She didn't like them. She would let her brother Adam have this one. He collected dolls. He had shelves and shelves and shelves of them, from the oldest doll that could only say "Mama" to the very latest model. He said he was going to be a father when he grew up.

She had saved her grandmother's present for last. It was her grandmother who truly understood her. Rebecca crossed her fingers and made a wish. If only her grandmother had remembered her promise. And how could she have forgotten, anyway? Rebecca had managed to mention it every time they talked.

The box from her grandmother was as wide as the cycle box but longer. Rebecca put off opening it. What if it wasn't . . . ?

She waited until the city speakers chirped the breakfast song at her.

> *Breakfast is a special meal,*
> *Gives your day get-up appeal.*
> *Eat your soybean egg all up,*
> *Finish with a cof-milk cup.*

"Yuch," Rebecca called back at the speaker. She only liked Solar Day breakfasts, those once-a-year feasts that happened when the sun truly cut through the smog. Solar Day breakfasts were soycakes and berry-milk.

The big birthday box seemed to stare at her. Rebecca could stand it no longer. She tore off the recycled paper. She ripped open the box top. She reached in and touched metal. She lifted out . . . a robot.

"She remembered!" shouted Rebecca. "Grandma remembered!"

"Of course I remembered." Grandma's beloved face came over the vid-phone. "And even if your parents don't approve of a robot for a child," she said, "I do. This one is factory programmed for a pre-teen owner. And I know you are old enough to keep it clean, pick up after it, and change its computer tape once a week."

"Oh, I will, I will. I promise," Rebecca said to her grandmother's image. She put her hand over her heart. Then she picked up the robot and held him up to the vid-phone. He was very heavy.

Grandma winked at Rebecca. "After all," she said, "you have been wanting a robot since you were two years old." Then her image faded and clicked off.

Rebecca blew a kiss at the empty screen. Then she turned to examine the robot. Grandma was wrong about one thing— Rebecca had wanted a robot since she was *one* year old. But who was counting now?

2

First Things First

Rebecca looked at her robot for a long time. She almost memorized him, from his shiny silver face-plate to the ball-bearing bottoms of his feet. She ran her fingers lightly over his black-and-chrome push buttons. Longingly, she looked at the instruction booklet hanging from his wrist by a copper wire. But at last she stood up and sighed.

"First things first," she reminded herself, and buzzed her brother's room.

"Yes?" he said at last, his snub-nosed image appearing green, then flesh-colored on the vid-phone.

"It's Rebecca."

"Of course it is," said Adam. He liked to think he had a high intuition rating, but Rebecca knew that he only tested average. "What do you want?"

"Permission to talk face-to-face," said Rebecca. "I have a surprise for you."

Adam stuck out his tongue at the screen. He hated face-to-facing. He especially hated being close enough to be touched. Rebecca often wondered how Adam could possibly become a father. Fathers were *supposed* to touch their children three times a day, whether they needed it or not. That's what the city speakers advised.

Rebecca held up the doll so the screen could close-focus on it.

"What's that?" asked Adam.

"A birthday present," said Rebecca.

"My birthday's not 'til April."

"Not *your* birthday. Mine." Rebecca pushed a button under the doll's arm. It burped and put its plastic hand over its plastic mouth. "Excuse me," it said, but its lips never moved.

"I want it!" shouted Adam, clapping his hands. *His* lips moved a lot.

"Then you'll have to face-to-face," said Rebecca.

Adam's picture left the screen abruptly and a door in Rebecca's wall slowly opened inward. "Come in," said Adam. "But remember, no hugging."

Rebecca went in. She had to step over parts of dolls. Everywhere on Adam's floor and table and bed were plastic arms, legs, heads.

"They're all apart," said Rebecca in surprise.

"That's because I've decided not to be a father when I grow up," Adam explained.

"You're going to be a junk collector instead?"

"No, a doctor." He brushed three legs off the chair. "So I have to know how things work. Put it here," he said.

Rebecca put the doll on the chair and pushed the doll's button. It burped twice, excusing itself both times.

"What do you want in trade?" asked Adam.

Rebecca said nothing for a moment. She pretended to think, but she had already decided what she would say. She scratched under each of her three braids in turn. Then she smoothed the bib of her coveralls. "Just answer my vid-phone when it rings and tell Mom and Dad that I'm with you, working. Can't be disturbed. And keep doing that 'til I tell you to stop."

Adam ran a hand through his unruly curly hair. "All right," he said at last, reluctantly. "But what will you be doing?"

"I'll let you know if it works out. And thanks." She gave Adam a quick hug.

"You promised no hugs!" he shouted. "Ich, yuch, pooey. Peh, peh, peh," he pretended to spit.

The wall speaker interrupted, chirping at them brightly:

Children, children, do not fight,
Sibling rivalry's not right.
Kiss and make up right away,
Or you'll have a dreary day.

"Oh keep quiet," Adam and Rebecca said to the speaker. Then they smiled at each other, gave the two-thumbs-up salute, and Rebecca left.

The sounds of doll-burping faded as she closed the door.

3

Second Things Next

Rebecca put the robot on her bed and patted the silver head lovingly. "Second things next," she reminded herself.

She printed a sign on the back of the robot's box and put it next to the robot.

DO NOT TOUCH
PRIVAT PROPETTY
THIS MEANS <u>YOU</u>,ADAM!!

Then she took the solar cycle from its carton and wheeled it into the street.

Their apartment-city was the largest metroplex in the East, but Rebecca knew her own sector well. Unlike her birthmates, she liked to walk about the streets instead of just memorizing facts in front of her vid-screen. Rebecca headed down the North-North corridor toward Snargriffid's room.

Snargriffid, usually called Snar by his/her friends, had always wanted a sunbike. That's because he/she came from Sizzlegrid IV, a planet that had lots of space to ride in and a sun that shone twenty-two hours a day. Someday Snar and his/her parent would be going back to Sizzlegrid, and he/she wanted to go back with a cycle.

As Rebecca wheeled the cycle, she listened to the sounds of the apartment-city at work. She heard the clankings of the garbage-bots as they ate trash, turning it

into heat for all the rooms. She listened to the trickle of water down the mecho-holes as corridor after corridor flushed itself clean. She heard the hum-buzz of the veggie-lites in the grow-cery store. Above all was the ever-present voice of the city speakers. The one closest to Rebecca was singing:

Right of way is for the fast,
Stay to the right and you'll be passed.
Move to the left and you can go
Past anyone who goes too slow.

"*Slowly,*" Rebecca corrected automatically. She was studying grammar on her vid-screen. People who could not pass grammar went into such jobs as writing speaker-songs.

Rebecca loved the sounds of her apartment-city. She could tell if something was wrong by the sound and could report it at once. Reporting mecho-breaks was the second thing a child learned in the apartment-city, after her own name and room number.

Snar's room was North-North-West 1776/2, the alien sector. It took five minutes to get there. Rebecca was careful not to bump into anyone as she wheeled her cycle along. Mornings were usually quiet times in the apartment-city. Grownups were at their work computers or outside jobs and children were studying at their vid-screens. But there were always a few people in the halls.

Just before she got to Snar's room, Rebecca had to flatten herself against the wall to let a large Efflerump by. Efflerumps lived on a planet where the gravity was very high and so they were very wide and spongy. They tended to take over an entire street, bouncing and flopping in Earth's lower gravity.

"Thank you," said the Efflerump as it passed, its voice thin. Rebecca could hear it mumbling more thank-yous as it continued

on its way. On Earth, Efflerumps were the politest of aliens. At *their* size, it was a good thing.

Rebecca pushed the cycle up to Snar's door and touched the buzzer. It echoed hollowly inside. "Hello . . . hello . . . hello . . . a visitor . . . isitor . . . tor."

Suddenly the door opened and there was Snargriffid, a four-foot-high insectoid, waving his/her antennae and smiling toothlessly.

"A glorious welcome to my most valued girl friend, Becca," said Snar. Sizzlegridians talked more than earth humans because they had to fill up their twenty-two hours of daylight somehow. Their nights were only two hours long.

"Hello," said Rebecca. "Want to trade?"

4

Want to Trade?

Snar put two hands up above his/her antennae and two hands in a prayer position by his/her mouth. Rebecca recognized it at once. It was the Sizzlegridian way of reminding someone about his/her manners.

"Oh, sorry," said Rebecca. "Hello valued boy/girl friend, Snargriffid." (It wasn't that Rebecca couldn't guess whether Snar was male or female. Sizzlegridians came in just one sex.) "It has been an overlong passage of time since we last talked."

"Not *talked*. Had adequate conversational sustenance," murmured Snar.

"Had adequate . . . oh, enough, Snar. You know what I mean," said Rebecca impatiently. "Want to trade?"

Snar turned three shades of brown, one right after another. He/she covered his/her antennae and earholes with his/her two pairs of hands.

"Oh, bother," grumped Rebecca. She *knew* by his/her rapidly vibrating antennae that Snar had seen the cycle. And she knew that he/she was dying to trade for it. But Sizzlegridians were absolute *bugs* on manners. She giggled quietly at her own joke. In fact, Sizzlegridians were masters of manners. It was what made them such good lawyers and politicians. And it was because Snar's father/mother was both of these that Rebecca had thought of the trade. So she forced herself to slow down and begin again.

"Hello valued friend, Snargriffid," she said in the toneless way that Sizzlegridians

liked so much. "It has indeed been an overlong passage of time since last we had adequate conversational sustenance."

Snar smiled and waggled his/her hands.

"The hours pass slowly. The sun seems to halt in its path until the light again when I can reacquaint myself with my valued friend, Snargriffid. And partake of his/her wise words," Rebecca added.

"Terrific!" chittered Snar. "Let's trade."

Rebecca pushed the bike into Snar's

room, shaking her head. "I don't think I will ever understand you," she said.

"I'm just trying to act human," Snar answered. "Besides," and his/her antennae began their rapid vibrations again, "in Sizzlegrid we have to fill up time. Here time gallops along. So should language. Or, as you would have it, 'That's some bike!' "

"Try it," suggested Rebecca.

Snar climbed on slowly, enjoying each part of the new operation. Without sun, the bike had no power and just wobbled along when the rider pushed its pedals.

"Please, valued friend Rebecca, supply the power. Or, as you would have it, 'Push!' "

Rebecca got behind and pushed.

"Sssssss . . . ssssssss . . . ssssssss!" chittered Snar. "Allllooopassssssssso!"

Rebecca giggled.

"An old Sizzlegridic phrase. It means: Move along with extreme speed and excessive caution on the part of pedestrians. Or,

as you would have it, 'Giddyap and . . .' "
Snar turned his/her head to look backward,
" 'and look out!' "

"Look out yourself," yelled Rebecca as
they plowed into a desk. Bike, Snar, and
Rebecca went tumbling.

Snar, lying under the bike and a desk
lamp, said happily, "I esteem most highly
this solar-powered velocipede and desire it
above all terran things." He/she smiled
toothlessly. "Or as you would have it, 'I
love it and want it.' "

Rebecca picked the lamp and bike off
Snar's thorax and legs. She tried not to look
triumphant. "Then the trade's on."

"What do you desire, Rebecca?" asked
Snar.

"Only a book," said Rebecca, suddenly
blushing.

"And does my most valued friend esteem
one particular volume more than any
other?" asked Snargriffid in his/her very
best manner.

"I do," admitted Rebecca. "I want one special book."

"Oh?" Snar waited. Waiting was another Sizzlegridian specialty.

"One of your parent's, actually." Rebecca looked at the floor. "The book is called *The Art of Detection*."

"What is this art?" asked Snar. "Is it like pottery? Or weaving? Or drawing pictures of sunrises? We Sizzlegridians value highly pictures of sunrises."

Rebecca had the courage at last to look Snar right in the antennae. "It is finding lost things. Solving crimes. Being a detective," she said.

"Aha!" breathed Snar. "In Sizzlegrid we have a name for that. It is called *SSSiptssshthesssshtesssing*. It translates into . . ." and Snar giggled, "individual antennae. Or as you would have it, 'private eye.'"

"You got it," said Rebecca happily. "Let's trade!"

5

A Program for Watson

Rebecca walked home slowly, cradling the big, brown book on detecting in her arms. She went over all her computer lessons in her head.

She knew that a computer remembers something by holding it in a "register," the way a person might remember something by holding it in a pocket. Only the computer can find something in a register faster than anyone can empty a pocket, sometimes in about a billionth of a second. Rebecca knew all this from her vid-screen lessons with Dr.

Dews. He called computers "machines to reckon with." But the computer knew only what was put into it. It could not make guesses about things it hadn't already been told. She would have to make sure she put all the proper stuff in the robot's computer so the robot could help her solve crimes. It would be a walking, talking helper. A computer with legs. And, if the detecting book was any help, a computer with legs that could solve crimes.

At her own door, still thinking about the robot, she held her hand up to the keyhole, palm forward. The houselock read her palmprint and let her in. She closed the door behind her and was back in her room before she even realized where she was.

The robot lay, untouched, staring up at her with blank eye scanners.

She opened the book and began to read aloud. "The world's most famous detective never really lived, except on the pages of a book and in the hearts of readers everywhere. His name was Sherlock Holmes, and his companion in solving crimes was Dr. Watson."

Rebecca looked up. She smiled at the robot, "Then, if I am going to be the world's second most famous detective and you are going to be *my* companion, it's elementary. I'll name you Watson II."

She reached over and detached the instruction booklet from his wrist. "PUSH *ON* BUTTON" was the booklet's first instruction. Rebecca pushed the robot's bright red *On* button. The second instruction read "PUSH *NAME* BUTTON. SPELL OUT NAME ON APPROPRIATE KEYS." Rebecca found the orange *Name* button and then punched the keys that relayed the robot's name to his memory bank.

"Hello Watson II," she said, "you may call me Sherlock Holmes." She pushed his green *Start* button.

Lights played across the register bank on the robot's chest. From behind his metal face came a voice, as high as a child's, but piercing. Every word had the same tone. "Hello, Sherlock Holmes," the robot said.

Rebecca giggled. "In public you'd better call me Becca."

Just then the city speaker called out the time:

Munch and munch
It's time for lunch,
Please don't forget your greens . . .

But Rebecca was so engrossed in her programming, she forgot not only her greens but her lunch as well. By dinnertime, Watson II knew as much about the art of detecting as anyone else in her sector, Rebecca thought. Maybe as much as anybody else in the whole apartment-city. Some programs had already been keyed into him at the robot factory—the ordinary dictionary and encyclopedia information that *all* robots had to have. Rebecca was sure that Watson II would be the best helper a detective could ever want.

Sitting at dinner, Rebecca gave her father two of his three touches before and after the soy stew: one hug and one armpit tickle. Over a delicious soy birthday cake sent by the apartment-city, Rebecca smiled at her brother, thanked her mother, and threw a kiss at her father. Thrown kisses were not considered touches. Then Rebecca went to bed early.

"She must be sick," mumbled her father to her mother.

"I've never seen her this way," admitted her mother.

They did the dishes together, breaking them happily and throwing the pieces into the chute for the garbage-bots. They talked with Adam far into the evening.

But Rebecca did not even read in bed or listen to her soothe-a-sleep. She fell asleep right away, knowing that meant she would wake up early, very early. Then she and the robot could go out into the streets of the metroplex and solve all the unsolved crimes they could find.

6

Looking for a Crime

Morning dawned. There was little sun, as usual, but no one doubted it was morning. The city speakers made that quite clear.

Morning dawns, the day is started.
Get up, wash up, get hair parted,
Socks on, teeth brushed, shoes tied, eat.
Make each day a special treat.
Ta-Taaaaaaa. Ta-Taaaaaaaaaaaa.

The speakers sang it twice, just in case anyone dared to dawdle in bed. But Rebecca was already up, washed, socked, brushed, parted, tied, and on her way to the cook-wall.

She dialed breakfast, which fell out of a slot and onto her plate. She didn't even make a face at the soybean egg, and she was finished well before the breakfast song was piped from the speakers. She threw the plate, fork, and cup down the garbage-hole.

"Now to solve some crimes," she said. She set Watson on the floor, programmed him for walking, opened the door, and they went out into the street.

Watson matched Rebecca step for step, though hers were light and happy and his a steady roll. The ball-bearings on the bottoms of his metal feet made a pleasant mechanical whirr.

Rebecca looked all around as they walked. She was searching for some sign that a crime had taken place. She checked flushlanes for stolen wallets. She listened down corridors for screams. She peeked through store windows, hoping to catch a thief at work. But the apartment-city was quietly clinking and clanking away, free of criminals or crime.

"Bother," said Rebecca, once to herself and once out loud.

"*Bother* does not compute," recited Watson in a monotone, his lights blinking on and off rapidly.

Rebecca turned and pushed two buttons on Watson's keyboard that meant "Shut up" in computer language, but weren't quite that polite. Watson was quiet, but he continued to follow her with his purring roll.

Six blocks, six long blocks, and two major crossroads, and Rebecca was getting angry. And hungry. They turned onto a seventh block and heard a small whimpering sound.

"Do you hear that?" whispered Rebecca to Watson.

The robot waved his metal arms at her but said nothing.

Rebecca turned for a moment, stopped, put her hands on her hips, and started to get mad at the mechanical man. "You are supposed to answer me when I ask a question," she said. Then she remembered. She had keyed him to shut up. Quickly she pushed his green *Start* button.

"I hear that," monotoned the robot.

They went toward the sound. The robot's infrared eye scanners checked the area, but it was Rebecca who found the source of the sound. It came from in front of a travel agency window full of posters for such faraway places as Sinistar, Meteor IX, Alpha Moonbase, and San Francisco.

"It's a baby," Rebecca said, kneeling beside a two-year-old dressed in a pinafore,

bonnet, and tiny sneakers. "A little girl," she added.

Gold curls peeked from under the baby's cap. She was crying and rubbing her eyes.

Rebecca looked up and down the street. She peered into the travel agency window. But she saw no one who looked like a mother or father. She knelt down and touched one of the baby's hands. "Can we help?" she asked.

The child looked up at the touch. Tears still ran from her eyes, but she gave Rebecca a gloriously wide smile.

"This is not a baby but a child," intoned Watson. "*Baby* is the designation of a pre-walking infant."

"Daddy!" cooed the child, holding up her hands to Watson. When he failed to hold out his arms, the child toddled over to him and held on to his knees.

"*Daddy* does not compute. It does not make sense. It is illogical," said Watson rigidly, but his memory-bank lights blinked rapidly from pink to red as if he were blushing.

"If she thinks you are her daddy," said Rebecca thoughtfully, looking up and down the street once again, "then she must be looking for her daddy. And if she's looking for her daddy—"

"Then it is logical to assume that either the child or the daddy is lost," finished Watson in his monotone. "Or abandoned. Left. Set out in the forest for wolves." He bent over jerkily and picked up the child.

In the robot's arms the child cooed happily and played with his push buttons, scrambling his answers.

Rebecca looked at the child. For the first time, she noticed the little girl had a piece of paper pinned to the back of her pinafore. The paper was covered with regular black spots.

"Lost child. That's a sort-of crime," said

Rebecca happily. "Or abandoned. Or left. Of course no one sets out children in the forests for wolves any more, Watson. That's just in the old old tales. There haven't been any wolves around for years. Or forests. So she must be lost." Rebecca smiled.

The child pushed more of his buttons and Watson replied, "We seven candles measle often taradiddle."

Rebecca looked into the child's incredible blue eyes. "What's your name, little girl?" she asked. "What is your room number?"

"Daddy," responded the lost child. She snuggled down in Watson's arms and fell asleep at once.

7

The Code-Carrying Kid

Rebecca did not touch the child sleeping in Watson's arms, but she quickly pushed his *Re-set* button.

"What do you think of this paper?" she asked, holding it up to his scanners.

"It is made of recycled wood pulp," he said.

Rebecca shook the paper twice. "Not that way. I mean the funny black marks. Did someone's pen give out? Is it a design? Or does it mean something?"

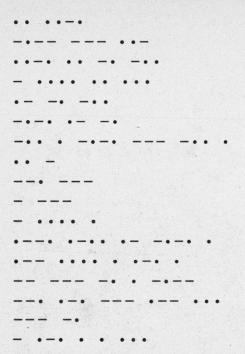

```
.. ..-.
-.-- --- ..-
.-. .. -. -..
- .... .. ...
.- -. -..
-.-. .- -.
-.. . -.-. --- -.. .
.. -
--. ---
- ---
- .... .
.--. .-.. .- -.-. .
.-- .... . .-. .
-- --- -. . -.--
--. .-. --- .-- ...
--- -.
- .-. . . ...
```

Watson hummed and buzzed for a minute. Inside his metal head, gears moved, transistors flickered, sorted, processed. Finally he said with a metallic sigh, "That is Morse code."

"Morse code!" Rebecca breathed. She

smiled and pulled on two of her braids. Then she frowned. "What's that?"

Watson gave a quick monotone lecture. "A code is a way of writing a message so that it can be understood by someone who knows the secret or key to its form. Putting messages into code is called cryptology. Morse code was invented by the American artist Samuel Finley Breese Morse in the nineteenth century. It is a code that uses a series of dots and dashes instead of letters."

As Watson continued his lecture, a small crowd of tourists began to gather. There were two Venusian swamp people who carried bits of their swamp in smelly backpacks to remind them of home. There was a rather large Sizzlegridian who was wearing a cowboy hat three sizes too small for his/her head. His/her antennae stuck out through holes in the brim. Three dragon masters from the McCaffrey Nebula, with tiny dragons riding on their shoulder pads, stopped to listen as well. They were all scattered by a passing Efflerump who flopped by muttering thank-yous to anyone within hearing distance.

Watson continued his lecture even though no one but Rebecca was still interested. As the child continued sleeping in Watson's arms, he discharged a printout sheet of Morse code for Rebecca from the slot in his belly:

THE CODE

A	•—	I	••	Q	——•—	Y	—•——
B	—•••	J	•———	R	•—•	Z	——••
C	—•—•	K	—•—	S	•••		
D	—••	L	•—••	T	—		
E	•	M	——	U	••—		
F	••—•	N	—•	V	•••—		
G	——•	O	———	W	•——		
H	••••	P	•——•	X	—••—		

Rebecca ripped off the printout and studied it. Then she slowly began to spell out the message.

"I . . . F . . . Y . . . O . . . U . . . F . . . I . . . N . . . D . . . T . . . H . . . I . . . S . . . A . . . N . . . D . . . oh bother," said Rebecca. "At this rate it will take forever. You do it." She held the message up to Watson's eye scanners.

Two seconds later another printout chattered from his belly:

IF YOU FIND THIS AND CAN DECODE IT
GO TO THE PLACE WHERE MONEY GROWS
ON TREES

"That does not compute," intoned Watson. He began to rock the child.

Rebecca looked thoughtful. She closed her eyes. Then suddenly she opened them— wide. "I think I know what it means!" she said.

A Second Crime

Rebecca crumpled up the message into a little ball and threw it in the nearby flushlane. Then she started to trot down the walk.

Watson rolled after her, mumbling over and over again, "That message does not compute. There is no logical explanation."

Braids flying, Rebecca turned a corner at North-North-East. She stopped in front of a well-lit window. Where Watson finally caught up with her. The child in his arms was still asleep. A white milk bubble was on her lips.

"That message does not compute. There is

no logical explanation," he complained mechanically.

"Maybe it's not logical to a robot," said Rebecca excitedly. "But you and your computer can only move from one bit of programmed information to another. A human mind can make strange leaps. And those leaps are often right. Look!"

"What you have said still does not compute," said Watson. But at Rebecca's command, he turned his scanners in the direction of her pointing finger.

In the window of the grow-cery store were various veg/fruits under grow-lites. The prices for the exotic foods were printed under the vines and trees:

$ 7.29 a pound for carratoes
$ 3.37 a bunch for bananaus
$ 5.26 a piece for cauliberries

"*Here's* where money grows on trees," said Rebecca. "Those veg/fruits cost much more than any regular soybean meal. Sometimes my grandmother gets me a veg/fruit for a special treat."

"I will store that in my memory cells," said Watson.

The child in his arms began to squirm. When she started squealing, Watson put her down and patted her gently on the head. At his touch, the child ran away, past the automatic eye of the store door. The doors opened, and the child ran through, out of sight.

"Don't let that kid get away," Rebecca cried out. "She's our first crime!" Rebecca charged ahead, with Watson at her heels.

As the door opened for them, an Efflerump flumped out and knocked them both down.

"Thank you," it said as it stepped on them. "Thank you."

Rebecca was up first, and helped Watson to his feet. She dusted off his lights and pushed his *Re-set* button.

"*Excuse me* would have been the proper exclamation," intoned Watson, bright red lights flashing crankily across his panel.

Rebecca yanked his hand. "Never mind," she said.

They went into the store.

"You take that aisle. I'll take this one. Find that child," Rebecca ordered.

She was halfway between the brocapples

and the cherryumbers when she saw the pinafored child sitting on a shelf. "Come here, kid," Rebecca called, grabbing her. With the squirming child under one arm, Rebecca walked to the front of the store. She looked around and saw Watson coming down the next aisle. She looked again. *He* was holding the child in *his* arms!

"Oh no!" called out Rebecca. "Which one is ours?"

"Daddy!" yelled the child Rebecca was holding. She twisted away from Rebecca and ran to Watson. Both children wore pinafores and bonnets and tiny sneakers. They were identical.

"Twins!" said Rebecca. "And look! The second one has a note pinned to the back of her shirt as well."

"Illogical," complained Watson as he tried to rock both squirmers to sleep. "Highly illogical."

Following a Clue

If you wish no food today,
Be polite and go away.
Grow-cery stores are meant for selling,
Not for talking, or for yelling.

"I know, I know," Rebecca mumbled at the city speakers. "We were just leaving."
The speakers heard her answer and replied with a cheerful:

Bye-bye, come again once more
To your friendly grow-cery store. . . .

The door shut behind them, cutting off the rest of the speakers' final message.

"Now, who would have figured on twins?" asked Rebecca, more to herself than to Watson.

But Watson responded automatically. "Twins. The probabilities for multiple births occuring are as follows: Twins, one in 96 births. Triplets, one in 9,216 births. Quadruplets, one in 884,736 births. Quintuplets, one in . . . ."

"Enough!" shouted Rebecca. "Let's work on this message. I bet it's in code, too. But it sure isn't Morse code. It's all a jumble of letters." She held the paper up to Watson's scanners. The first child grabbed the paper and with a high-pitched little laugh, threw it into the air.

A gust from the grow-cery store cooling system blew the paper even higher.

"Oh no," cried Rebecca. "Come back."

"I have not gone anywhere," said Watson.

"Not you, idiot. The message." Rebecca desperately kept her eyes on the paper, which floated high above her head. It blew from gust to gust along the wall.

"Illogical," said Watson. "Paper cannot respond to a command."

But Rebecca was not listening to him. Instead she was following the paper message as it floated around the corner and down the street. Watson stayed where he was, holding the two babies. Rebecca had not commanded him to come along.

As Rebecca ran, she bumped first into an old man from Chameleon II who was sitting on the corner, disguised as a fire hydrant. She knew he was a man and not a hydrant because he was drinking a soda. And the hydrant had a thatch of white hair. People from Chameleon II were very good at blending into their backgrounds, but there

was always something just a little wrong
with their disguises.

Rebecca rammed into a couple from a
water planet who walked around with fish
tanks full of liquid covering their heads.
They yelled at her in Bubble-talk.

She pushed aside an Efflerump in her

haste, and it was so startled that it forgot to say "Thank you" and couldn't eat for a week due to shock.

Just as Rebecca turned the corner of North-North-West 1700s, her eyes still on the paper floating high overhead, there was a screech of brakes and the helpless shriek, "Allllooopasssssssso!"

Rebecca felt herself lifted up and thrown into the air. She grabbed for the paper, missed, tumbled over, and landed on the sidewalk. Hard.

"Why don't you look where you're going?" she screamed, half in anger, half in fear.

Then she looked up, and standing over her was Snargriffid. He/she was turning from brown to red over and over and over again.

"Oh dear, oh dear, oh dear," Snar was saying. "Oh my dear nearly departed and much admired friend, Rebecca. Oh, forgive my ineptitude on this solar-powered veloci-pede. It has an unfortunate tendency not to slow its forward progress when the braking mechanism is applied by insectoid feet. Did you not hear me vocalize a warning before impaction? I believe your antennae were committed elsewhere at the time. Oh dear. Oh dear."

"In other words," said Rebecca to her friend as she painfully scrambled to her feet, "you don't know how to use the brakes yet and yelled. I wasn't looking. And we crashed."

"You got it!" said Snar, giving a particularly toothless smile.

He/she brushed Rebecca's coveralls off and straightened her three braids. Together they put the cycle upright again.

Snar mounted his/her bike. "What were you looking at anyway?"

"Oh, bother," said Rebecca, suddenly remembering. "My message."

"Message?" Snar looked as puzzled as an insectoid could.

"A piece of paper with some writing on it. I have to figure out what it means," explained Rebecca.

"Oh," said Snar. "Perhaps you mean *that* bit of recycled wood pulp lying against the wall?" He/she pointed to a piece of crumpled paper.

"Oh, yes," Rebecca breathed thankfully. She raced over to the wall and leaned down to pick it up. At that very moment, the flushlane swooshed gallons of antiseptic water through and washed the paper away. It whirled down a mecho-hole and out of sight.

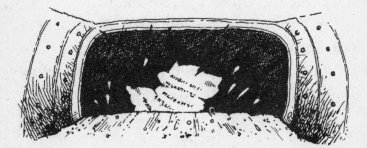

Do not litter, do not trash,
Cleaning up takes lots of cash . . . .

warned the speakers.

"I know, I know," said Rebecca to the ground. She started back toward the growcery store where she had left Watson and the twins. Behind her, pushing his/her bike, came Snar calling softly in his/her chittering voice: "Can I be of assistance, friend Rebecca? Hey, Becca, can I help?"

10

The Second Message

Watson was waiting at the grow-cery store, his red lights blinking on and off. He was singing "A Bicycle Built for Two" to the twins in a mechanical way. They were fast asleep in his arms.

Rebecca came up to him and stood for a minute. There were tears brimming in her eyes. She didn't even bother to wipe them away. She snuffled. "Some detective. I lost the secret message down a flushlane. My whole detective life went down the drain, too."

Watson kept on singing.

"Don't you care?" Rebecca suddenly shouted at Watson.

"Computers are not built for caring," intoned Watson. "We are built for solving problems."

Rebecca looked unhappily at the twins asleep in the robot's arms. "You sure seem to be caring for *them,*" she mumbled. "You were singing."

"I have been programmed at the factory to sing that one song," said Watson. "It seems to solve the problem of squirming children."

"Oh," said Rebecca with a sniff.

"Besides," monotoned Watson, "I think they like it."

"What *I'd* like," Rebecca said softly, "is to have my message back again."

Watson's lights blinked rapidly. Inside his head, gears meshed. In less than twenty seconds, a paper slid out of the slot in his belly. "As you wish," said Watson.

"But how? What? I mean, why?" Rebecca tried, then gave up. She tore off the paper and held it to her heart.

"You showed the message to me before the child threw it into the air. I scan all messages instantly. I store all data in my memory banks unless commanded not to," said Watson.

For once Rebecca was speechless.

"Allllooopasssssssso!" came a cry from behind her.

"Not again," moaned Rebecca and jumped to one side.

Snargriffid slammed into the wall.

Rebecca helped her friend up, but the cycle was bent in funny places.

"It appears to be more satisfactory," said Snar with a sigh, "when the cycle propels itself into a piece of anatomy instead of a piece of masonry. Or, as you would have it, 'People make softer landings than walls.'"

"Watson will fix it. Won't you?" asked Rebecca.

"I will see to it after we solve this mystery," replied Watson.

Snar laughed. It was a high, tuneful chitter.

Rebecca looked at the message.

HE XNT EHMC SGHR ZMC BZM CDBNCD HS EM
RM NJYAC UFCPC ZYZGCQ EPMU GL ZMVCQ

As Rebecca looked at the message, Watson's belly slot began to feed out another message. "Here is the key to the code," he said.

ABCDEFGH I JKLMNOPQRSTUVWX YZ
ZABCDEFGH I JKLMNOPQRSTUVWX Y
YZABCDEFGH I JKLMNOPQRSTU VWX

"I don't get it," said Rebecca. "Can't you explain?"

Watson's lights flashed cheerily, red then green then red again. "This is a slightly more difficult code," intoned Watson. "The Morse code was a simple letter-substitution code, dots and dashes for each letter. This code has two substitutions. The first line of the message is decoded using the second alphabet. The next line uses the third alphabet."

"I am thoroughly confused," sighed Snar.

Rebecca sat down on the sidewalk and crossed her legs. She tugged at one of Snar's hands, and the Sizzlegridian sat down next to her. He/she crossed his/her legs and folded one pair of hands up over his/her head and the other under his/her chin.

"Now look," said Rebecca patiently. "In the message's first line, the letter *A* will be written as *Z*. But in the second line of the message it will be written as *Y*."

Snar traced the substitutions with his/her hand on the paper. "Oh," he/she said at last, "sunshine rises over the rim of the farthest hills. Or, as you would have it, 'Light dawns!' "

"Good," said Rebecca. "Let's figure out this one."

Snargriffid began to spell excitedly, "I . . . F . . . Y . . . O . . . U . . . F . . . I . . . N . . . D . . ."

Watson's voice cut across their slow decoding. "If you find this and can decode it, go to place where babies grow in boxes." He whirred and buzzed for a full minute, then added, "That is highly illogical. Babies grow in test tubes. Every computer knows that."

11

Dead End

Rebecca sat with her chin on her hands. She said nothing.

Snar, who could not stand silences, began to talk. "Of course, on Sizzlegrid babies grow neither in boxes nor in test tubes but rather develop in egg cases on the parent's back."

Rebecca did not seem to hear.

"On McCaffrey the dragons are born singly in eggs. And I understand that on the planetoid of Omega/Omicron, teeth are sown like seeds in rows and armed warriors rise up like wheat."

"I know what it means!" Rebecca shouted suddenly, ignoring her friend. Her voice rang down the street, startling two tourists from the dark side of the moon where there was never any noise at all.

> *Do not yell and do not shout,*
> *There are other folk about . . .*

began the city speakers, but Rebecca was already up and running down the street. At the corner, she checked the map etched into the side of the building. Using her finger, she traced the quickest route.

"Follow me," she called over her shoulder to Snargriffid, who was dragging his/her twisted cycle. At the command, Watson began to roll after them, the twins still cradled in his arms.

They made two left turns and three rights. They crossed one main highway.

Rebecca used the *Run* lane. Watson used the *Roll* lane. Snar, because of the cycle, used the *Hobble* lane. Next to them, the three lanes marked *Crawl, Hop,* and the water lane marked *Swim* were empty. But overhead the *Fly* lanes were crowded with a tour group from the Eagle Six galaxy.

"Which direction are we perambulating in?" Snar shouted.

Rebecca kept on going.

"Or as you would have it, 'Where are we going?' " called the insectoid.

But they were already there. Up ahead, Rebecca had stopped and pressed her nose against a glass window in the wall. She was pointing.

Watson rolled to a stop. Snargriffid arrived at last and dumped the broken cycle by their feet.

"Look!" said Rebecca.

Inside the window were a variety of dolls lying in boxes. There were pink-skinned dolls, black-skinned dolls, red-skinned dolls, and an insectoid doll as well. It looked like a miniature Sizzlegridian.

"I was never *that* small," said Snar.

"Improbable," intoned Watson.

"We'll see," said Rebecca. "I'm a pretty good detective, you know."

Just then a fat man with a big cigar in his mouth stepped out of the door of the doll store. The cigar steamed and the man patted his big belly. "Well, well, well," he said, and his cigar puffed. "Well, well, well."

Rebecca stepped up to him. "Are you missing two kids? Twins? If so, I have found them. They had messages pinned to their pinafores. They think my robot is their daddy. I'm a detective, you know."

"Improbable, illogical, and unproved," added Watson.

The man patted his belly again and looked up at the sky where the haze lifted

for a moment and a patch of blue could be seen. Then the smoke from his cigar blotted out the blue sky as easily as a cloud. "Well, well, well," he said. His tone never changed.

"Well, well, well, yourself," said Rebecca, beginning to lose her temper and her manners. "Well, are they yours?"

Snar gasped.

The big man smiled and puffed once more. Then he looked down at Rebecca. "Well, well, well," he said.

"Oh, *please*," Rebecca began, close to tears. But the big man ignored her and looked again at the sky. "And I thought I had it," Rebecca mumbled. She turned to Watson and Snar. "I guess I'm *not* a good detective after all. Not a good detective or a good anything." She turned to go home.

Watson said nothing.

Snar, who came from a desert planet where wasting water was forbidden, still could not help the tiny tear of sympathy that beaded the tip of his/her antennae. "Oh, Rebecca . . ." he/she began and then stopped. Watson was correct. There was nothing that could be said.

12

Big and Little

"Wait!" came a small voice.

Thinking that the big man had changed his mind—and his voice as well—Rebecca turned. Then she stared. From behind the big man stepped a small man. He was not much taller than Rebecca. He had a beard and was dressed in a white suit with a red tie and handkerchief. Smile lines surrounded his eyes.

"Wait," he said again in his light, smily voice. "And listen." He patted the larger man on the back.

The big man puffed his cigar. Wrapped in its smoke, he said, "Well, well, well."

The little man nodded. "I'm afraid that you have heard the beginning, middle, and end of Mr. Big's vocabulary. He's one of my early adult models. Conversation is not his strongest feature. What I was after when I made him was verisimilitude."

"Verisimilitude?" Rebecca had trouble pronouncing it. "What's that?"

"*Verisimilitude* means imitating life," intoned Watson.

"Exactly," said the little man. "Exactly. Mr. Big is nothing more than a doll. But he

is very lifelike. And that's my business. Lifelikely Dolls, Inc. Let me introduce myself." He reached into his pocket and pulled out a handkerchief and a card. With a bow, he presented the card to Rebecca. It had letters that seemed to glitter.

LIFELIKELY DOLLS, INC.
NNE 2700/24
Bosyork, America

"We create Life-like"

HARRY BARR DUSSELDWARF, *Prop.*

"And are you . . . ." Rebecca began.

"Yes, Harry Barr himself," said the little man. "But I know all about you and Watson and your Sizzlegridian friend." He bowed and waved the red handkerchief once again before popping it back into his pocket.

"Improbable," intoned Watson. "You could not know all about us."

Snar shook his/her head and waved his/her antennae in an agitated manner. "I must agree."

Rebecca put her head to one side. "How could you know *all* about me," she said.

"An excellent question from an excellent detective," said Mr. Dusseldwarf. "And it is true, I do not know *all* about you. Just *all* about you since you found my twins. They take in as well as give out."

Watson's panel lights ran a riot of colors to show he was confused. "Impossible. Improbable."

"Well, well, well," added Mr. Big at that moment.

Harry Barr Dusseldwarf smiled. "Haven't you guessed yet?" he asked. He took the little girls from Watson's arms, set them on the ground, and patted their heads.

"Daddy," they cried, and ran through Mr. Big's legs and into the store.

Watson stared ahead, a clanking echoing in his head.

"This puzzle is too difficult for a Sizzle-gridian mind," admitted Snar at last.

But Rebecca smiled back at Mr. Dusseldwarf. "They're dolls, of course," she said. "Dolls that you made, Mr. Dusseldwarf."

"Of course," agreed the little man. "Call me Harry Barr." He took her hand and led her into the store.

Inside there were tele-vid cameras and a giant cake. "You are the winner of the first annual Lifelikely Doll Advertising Puzzle," said the little man. "Better smile. You don't want to be frowning in your pictures."

13

Rebecca's Solution

"BIRTHDAY GIRL SOLVES NEW-DOLL PUZZLE," read the headline in the evening paper as it chattered out of the Newsfax slot by the dinner dispenser. The after-dinner tele-vid news would carry the story as well. Rebecca grinned as her father read it aloud to the family.

"*Rebecca Jasons, of 1700/37 NNE Bosyork was nine years old yesterday, and today she solved an advertising puzzle that stumped the older residents of our fair apartment-city. Finding two look-alike chil-*

dren in different parts of her sector (see map below), Ms. Jasons searched for the children's parents or home. The children, of pre-language age, could offer no help."

"That means," explained Rebecca, "that all they could say was 'Daddy.' "

"Ms. Jasons was aided by her faithful companion Watson, a robot, series # 1960gh483406745 (see circuitry below), and a Sizzlegridian friend, Snargriffid of the Mantisline (see family tree below).

"The twins, however, were neither true humans nor humanoids from another galaxy. They were, in fact, the latest creations of Harry Barr Dusseldwarf's well-known Lifelikely Dolls, Inc. (see projected income below). The two dolls were part of a citywide publicity campaign invented by the famous Mr. Dusseldwarf.

"The dolls, called Little Baby Runaway, look like two-year-olds. They sleep, cry, *and make bubbles just like many dolls on the market. But they also have a cleverly concealed button on the top of their heads, underneath a sunbonnet and curls. Pat them on the head (see patented plans below) and they run away from home.*

"Mr. Dusseldwarf placed three of the dolls in various parts of the city. They had coded messages pinned to their pinafores. There was a prize for their recovery. The third doll has yet to be found."

Mr. Jasons finished reading the article and looked up from the paper. "And you did it all by yourself," he said proudly. He reached over and patted Rebecca on the head.

"Watch out, Dad," warned Adam. "She might run away."

They all laughed.

Rebecca's mother, coming in late from work, asked, "What's so funny?"

"I'm a real true detective, Mom," said

Rebecca. "I solved a mystery, and what's more, I got a reward."

"A reward!" her mother exclaimed.

"You didn't mention *that,*" said Adam. "What was it?"

"Watson," Rebecca called into her room. "Bring in my reward."

Watson rolled in through the doorway, a child asleep in his arms. It was snoring lightly, a milk bubble on its lips.

"It's the latest Dusseldwarf Doll," said Rebecca.

"And those are *so* expensive," said her mother.

"Oh, I want it," cried Adam. "Are you giving that one to me, too?"

"No," said Rebecca. "I have given it to Watson."

The doll stirred in the robot's arms and cried out sleepily, "Daddy!"

Watson patted her clumsily on the head.

At once the baby sat up and squirmed

away from the robot. She crashed to the ground but was up on her feet in a moment. Before any of them could move, the doll was out the door.

"Bother!" said Rebecca.

"Double bother!" said Watson.

"Will someone explain all this to me?" said Rebecca's mother, dropping her briefcase onto the sofa and collapsing beside it.

Her father and Adam started to talk at once, but Rebecca ignored them. Instead she went over to Watson whose scanners were looking back and forth across his empty arms.

"Never mind," said Rebecca. "If we found her once, we can find her again."

"Your chances are one in 7,890,764," intoned Watson. He hesitated. "But with *my* help. . . ."

"You're on," said Rebecca, nudging him in the metal side with her elbow. "After dinner we'll get back to detecting."

Watson's panel of lights flashed merrily, and Rebecca could have sworn that she saw his eye scanners wink. Except, of course, *that* would have been highly illogical.

Jane Yolen, well-known for her fairy tale, science fiction, and fantasy stories, is the author of over fifty books for children. Also a lecturer, teacher, and critic, Ms. Yolen's articles have appeared in *The New York Times, Cricket, Horn Book, Language Arts, Childhood Education,* and *Fantasy & Science Fiction.*

Ms. Yolen received a B.A. from Smith College and an M.Ed. from the University of Massachusetts. She has been a recipient of the Christopher Medal, the Golden Kite Award, and a 1968 Caldecott Honor Book for *The Emperor and the Kite.* One of her books was nominated for the National Book Award.

Ms. Yolen lives in a farmhouse in Hatfield, Massachusetts with her husband, David Stemple, and their three children.